Walt Disney's Winnie the Pooh
The Merry Christmas Mystery

By Betty Birney
Illustrated by Nancy Stevenson

A GOLDEN BOOK • NEW YORK
Western Publishing Company, Inc., Racine, Wisconsin 53404

It was a very snowy night before Christmas. Winnie the Pooh was so excited, he had a hard time getting to sleep. He was thinking about the next day, when he and his friends would decorate the Great Pine Tree, then gather around it for their annual Christmas sing-along.

When he finally drifted off, Pooh dreamed of all the wonderful honey treats he was sure that Santa would bring him.

The next morning Pooh raced to his Christmas stocking. But instead of the honey treats he was hoping for, he found a very puzzling present.

"I wonder why Santa brought me thistles," said Pooh. "But they *are* very nice thistles. *Ah-choo!*"

Unfortunately, thistles made Pooh sneeze.

Pooh tried to get his mind off sneezing by practicing for the sing-along. He sang:

"Christmas is a time to share,
To show your friends how much you care . . .
"Ah-choo!" He sneezed again.

"A smackerel of honey will cure my sneezing," Pooh decided.
But when he went to the cupboard, all his jars were empty.
"Maybe Piglet will bring some honey when he stops by," Pooh
thought hopefully.

Just then there was a knock at the door. Pooh opened it and was startled by what he saw. Standing there was a mysterious creature with long orange fur and a large round head.

"Don't be scared, Pooh. It's me—Piglet," his small friend announced. "Santa brought me this coat for Christmas. It's a bit big, but it should keep me warm when we decorate the tree."

"It wouldn't happen to have any honey in the pockets, would it?" Pooh asked.

Piglet checked. There was no honey, only the haycorn ornaments he had made.

"That reminds me," said Pooh. "I have to take along *my* decoration for the Great Pine Tree."

Pooh took the chain of golden honey pots from the Christmas tree. Then he and Piglet rushed through the frosty white forest to meet their friends.

"Oops," said Piglet as he tripped over his long coat.

"Oh, bother!" said Pooh. "I guess Santa forgot your size."

When they arrived at the Great Pine Tree, Pooh wished Eeyore a Merry Christmas.

"How do you like the thistles Santa—*ah-choo!*—brought me?" Pooh asked.

"They're beautiful," Eeyore answered wistfully. "As beautiful as this coat rack Santa brought me."

Rabbit stepped forward. "That's not a coat rack, Eeyore. It's a very fine rake," he said admiringly.

Pooh noticed that Rabbit was wearing a tiny pair of earmuffs.

"Santa brought them," Rabbit explained.

"And I got this Tiggerific jar of honey!" said Tigger.

Pooh held his empty tummy and asked, "Does it taste good?"

"How would I know? Tiggers HATE honey," his bouncy friend replied. "But it was nice of Santa to think of me."

"Santa brought *me* something to eat, too," said Roo, showing his friends a jar of crunchy cookies.

"Do they have any honey in them?" Pooh asked hopefully.

"No," Roo said. "They're made of birdseed. They taste terrible. But Santa was nice to bring them."

"Santa sure left some very puzzling presents," said Piglet.

"It's a mystery," said Pooh. "But I like mysteries."

"Well, then," said Rabbit. "Here's another mystery for you. Where is Owl?"

"He's late," Piglet said.

"This *is* mysterious," Pooh agreed. "Owl is *never* late."

The friends decided to go ahead and start decorating the Great Pine Tree, because Owl's part in the ceremony always came last.

After they finished hanging their ornaments, they waited for Owl. Then they waited and waited and waited some more.

"I'm cold!" moaned Tigger.

"And I'm hungry!" groaned Pooh.

"Aw, here. Have some honey," said Tigger. Pooh gratefully accepted.

"If you're cold, Tigger, please take this coat," Piglet said.

"Gee, it fits perfectly!" exclaimed Tigger.

"And I'll bet these earmuffs would keep your ears warmer than mine," said Rabbit, placing the fuzzy earmuffs on Roo's ears.

Pooh was halfway through the pot of honey when he noticed Eeyore looking longingly at his thistles. "Would you like them, Eeyore?"

"Thanks for noticing me," said Eeyore, accepting his favorite treats. "I don't suppose anybody could use this coat rack, uh, I mean rake?"

Rabbit eagerly reached out for the tool. "Thank you, Eeyore," he said. "It's just what I wanted."

Roo looked down at the jar of birdseed cookies. "If anybody would like these cookies, I'd be happy to share them," he said.

"Oh, thank you, Roo!" said Owl, swooping down from a tree. He took a bite of one of the cookies and declared it to be delicious.

Then he said, "Sorry I'm so late. But I got lost on my way here!"

Owl's friends wondered how he could get lost in the Hundred-Acre Wood. "I'll show you," said Owl.

He led them a short distance to a road sign. "Here's the problem," said Owl. "These arrows are all mixed up, so I ended up going in the wrong direction."

The friends studied the signpost carefully. Sure enough, the arrow that should have been pointing to Owl's house was turned so it pointed to Eeyore's house.

And the arrow for Eeyore's house was pointed toward Pooh's house. In fact, all of the arrows were pointing the wrong way.

"The signpost must have gotten turned around in the snowstorm," said Rabbit.

Pooh scratched his head thoughtfully. "I think we've just solved our mystery."

"That's right!" said Piglet. "I'll bet Santa got confused and delivered our presents to the wrong houses."

"Do you mean these mittens aren't really for me?" Owl asked, pointing to a pair of small purple mittens hanging from a string around his neck.

"No, Owl. These birdseed cookies are for you," said Pooh. "Now, think, think, think. Who could these mittens be meant for?"

Piglet gently cleared his throat. *"A-hem."*

Owl smiled and handed the mittens to Piglet. "Of course, Piglet. They'll fit you much better."

After they straightened the sign, the friends returned to the Great Pine Tree. Soon Kanga arrived with hot chocolate and cakes and honey, as she did every year.

And Christopher Robin brought a beautiful, shiny star, as he did every year.

"I was hoping you'd come," said Pooh.

"I always do," Christopher Robin reminded him.

Owl flew the shiny star to the top of the tree, as he did every year.

Then, as a soft snow began to fall, the friends joined hands and sang:

"Christmas is a time to share,
To show your friends how much you care.
Whether they are big or small,
Friends are the very best gifts of all."

When the song was finished, Tigger said, "I hope Santa brings us some more puzzling presents next year so we can swap 'em again."

"Yes, it's nice to have a mystery for Christmas," Pooh explained. "As long as there's honey to go with it."

Christopher Robin chuckled and said, "Silly old bear."

Then he bent down and gave Pooh a special Christmas hug.